This collection first published 2003
by Walker Books Ltd
87 Vauxhall Walk
London SE11 5HJ

2 4 6 8 10 9 7 5 3 1

Text © year of publication individual authors
Illustrations © year of publication individual illustrators
Cover illustration © 2003 Melissa Sweet

Printed in China

British Library Cataloguing in Publication Data:
a catalogue record for this book is available from the British Library

ISBN 0-7445-8667-4

Love and Kisses

Ten Stories
to Share with Your
Little Loved Ones

WALKER BOOKS
AND SUBSIDIARIES
LONDON • BOSTON • SYDNEY

Contents

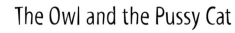

I Love Animals

Flora McDonnell

I love Jock,
my dog.

I love the ducks
waddling to
the water.

I love the hens
hopping up and down.

I love the goat
racing across the field.

I love the donkey
braying "hee-haw!"

I love the cow
swishing her tail.

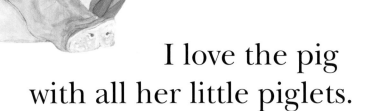

I love the pig
with all her little piglets.

I love the pony
rolling over and over.

I love the sheep
bleating to her lamb.

I love the cat
washing her kittens.

I love the turkey
strutting round
the yard.

I love all the animals…

I hope they love me.

WHO DO YOU LOVE?

Martin Waddell

illustrated by Camilla Ashforth

Holly played on the hillside each night,

until Mama called her in for her tea.

"Night-night!" Holly said.

"Night-night, Holly!" called her friends

and Holly went in.

"Bedtime now, Holly!" said Mama,

　when they had finished their tea.

"I want to play our go-to-bed game!" Holly said.

"Bed first, then the game," Mama said.

"I want to play while I'm getting ready for bed,"

　Holly said.

　And Mama started the game.

"Who do you love, Holly?" asked Mama.

"I love Grandpa," Holly said.

"He takes me for walks in the wood and he makes dandelion clocks for me. And I hide away where he can't see me. He says, 'Where are you, Holly?' Then I jump out and shout **BOO!**"

"Poor Grandpa!" said Mama.

"Now ask me again!" Holly said.

"Who do you love?" asked Mama.

"Let me think!" Holly said.

"I love Grandma because she makes big cakes at her house.
She stirs the mix and I put the cherries on top. Then I lick
the spoon. Grandma makes the best cakes in the wood."

"You'll get fat eating cakes," said Mama.

"I don't care!" Holly said. "I like Grandma's cakes."

Mama looked for the towel but Holly wanted

more of the game.

"Ask me who I love," Holly said. "Ask me again!"

"Who do you love?" asked Mama.

"I love Arthur," said Holly.

"I love Arthur because he is my brother. He lets me ride on his bike. Sometimes I ride down the hill and then I fall off in the grass at the bottom. Arthur says that's how you learn to ride bikes."

"I see!" said Mama.

"Ask me some more!" Holly said.

"Who do you love?" asked Mama.

"I love Pa because he is my Pa," Holly said. "He tells me
    stories all about my adventures."

"What sort of adventures?" asked Mama.

"I was a princess and I lived in a castle with Arthur. One day there was a dragon and Arthur didn't know what to do. I got some water and poured it all over the dragon and put his fire out. Pa says I saved Arthur, and I made the dragon my friend," Holly said.

"Who else do you love?" asked Mama.

"I think I've done everyone now," Holly said.

"You've left someone out!" said Mama.

 It was the part of the game that Holly liked best.

"Ask me again!" Holly said.

"Who do you love, Holly?" asked Mama.

"I love ... old Postman Cat because he brings us our letters," Holly said. "Just old Postman Cat?" asked Mama.

"I love ... Cousin Ollie who comes every Sunday," Holly said. "I love Cousin Ollie a lot!"

"I love ... the three kittens who roll down the hill," Holly said.

"I love ... the cat with the hat that we met yesterday in the wood," Holly said.

"I think I might cry!" sighed Mama.

"Don't cry, Mama," Holly said. "You just have to ask
me again."

"Who do you love, Holly?" asked Mama.

"I love you," said Holly.

"And I love you too," Mama said. "You know
that I do."

Mama hugged Holly and put her to bed,
and that was the end of the go-to-bed game.

Bunny My Honey

by Anita Jeram

Mummy Rabbit had a baby.

His name was Bunny.

He looked just like his mummy,

only smaller.

He had long ears,

a twitchy nose and great big feet.

"Bunny, my Honey,"
Mummy Rabbit liked to call him.

Mummy Rabbit showed Bunny how to

do special rabbity things,

like running and hopping,

digging and twitching his nose

and thumping his great big feet.

Sometimes Bunny played with his best friends,

Little Duckling and Miss Mouse.

They played quack-quacky games,

squeaky games and thump-thump-thumpy games.

They sang,   *We're the little Honeys.*
A little Honey is sweet.
Quack quack, squeak squeak,
Thump your great big feet!

If a game ever ended in tears,

as games sometimes do,

Mummy Rabbit made it better.

"Don't cry, my little Honeys,"
Mummy Rabbit said. "I'm right here."

But one day Bunny got lost.

Oh, how could such a bad thing happen?

Perhaps it was a game that went wrong.

Perhaps Bunny ran too far on his own.

But there he was, just one lost Bunny.

The more Bunny looked for

his friends and his mummy

the more lost

and the more lost

and the more lost he became.

Bunny started to cry.

"Mummy, Mummy,
I want my mummy!
Mummy, Mummy,
I want my mummy!"

"Bunny, my Honey!"

What was that?

"Bunny, my Honey!

Bunny, my Honey!"

"Bunny, my Honey!"

"MUMMY!"

Mummy Rabbit picked Bunny

up and cuddled him.

She stroked his long ears.

She put her twitchy nose

on his twitchy nose.

She kissed his great big feet.

Bunny's ears and nose

and feet felt warm all over.

"I love you, Mummy,"
Bunny whispered.
"I love you, Bunny, my Honey,"
Bunny's mummy
whispered back,
"and I love my other
little Honeys too."

On the way home, Bunny and Miss Mouse and Little Duckling sang their song.

We're the little Honeys.
A little Honey is sweet.
Quack quack, squeak squeak,
Thump your great big feet!

And Bunny was a
happy rabbit.

We Love Them

Martin Waddell   illustrated by Barbara Firth

In all the white fields there was one rabbit.

It was lost.

It was small.

It lay in the snow.

Ben found it.

Ben barked.

We picked it up and took it home.

Becky thought it would die, but it didn't.

It lay with Ben.

Ben licked it.

Becky said that Ben thought it was a little dog,

and it thought Ben was a big rabbit.

They didn't know they'd got it wrong.

Becky said we wouldn't tell them.

We called our rabbit Zoe.

She stayed with Ben.

She played with Ben.

We loved them.

Zoe wasn't little for very long.

She got big ...

and bigger ...

and bigger still,

but not as big as Ben.

But Ben was old ...

and one day Ben died.

We were sad and Zoe was sad.

She wouldn't eat her green stuff.

She sat and sat.

There was no Ben for our rabbit,

until one day …

in the pale hay …

there was a puppy.

We took it home.

It lay down with Zoe.

Becky said our puppy thought Zoe was a dog.

And Zoe thought our puppy was a rabbit.

They didn't know they'd got it wrong.

Becky said we wouldn't tell them.

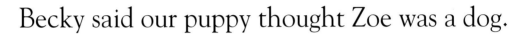

The puppy stayed.

The puppy played.

We loved him,

just like we loved Ben.

We called our puppy Little Ben.

But Little Ben got big ...

and bigger ...

and bigger still.

He got bigger than our rabbit

but not as big as old Ben.

Zoe still thinks Little Ben is a rabbit,

and Becky says that Zoe doesn't mind.

Becky says that Zoe likes big rabbits.

Zoe and Little Ben play

with us in the green fields.

They are our dog

and our rabbit.

We love them.

The Owl
and the
Pussy Cat

Edward Lear
illustrated by Louise Voce

The Owl
and the Pussy cat
went to sea
In a beautiful
pea-green boat,

They took some honey,
and plenty of money,
Wrapped up in a
five-pound note.

The Owl looked up
to the stars above,
And sang
to a small guitar,

"O lovely Pussy!
O Pussy, my love,
What a beautiful
Pussy you are,
You are, you are!
What a beautiful
Pussy you are!"

69

Pussy said to the Owl,
"You elegant fowl!
How charmingly
sweet you sing!
O let us be married!
too long we have tarried:
But what shall we
do for a ring?"

They sailed
away, for a year
and a day,

To the land where
the Bong Tree grows,

And there in a wood
a Piggy-wig stood
With a ring
at the end of his nose,
His nose, his nose,
With a ring
at the end of his nose.

"Dear Pig,
are you willing
to sell for one shilling
Your ring?"
Said the Piggy, "I will."

So they took it away,
and were married
next day
By the Turkey
who lives on the hill.

They dined on mince,
and slices of quince,
Which they ate
with a runcible spoon;

And hand in hand,
on the edge of the sand,
They danced
By the light of the moon,
The moon, the moon,
They danced
by the light of the moon.

IF YOU
LOVE A BEAR

PIERS HARPER

If you love a bear
you will know that bears
like to be woken up gently.

Then they jump out of bed
and run to the kitchen to make breakfast.

Bears eat a lot more
than children do.

If you love a bear
you will know
that bears don't
wear clothes.

They don't know
where to put them.

Instead they run races ...

and dance dances.

If you love a bear
you will know that
bears like being outside.

They find interesting
things ...

and play
peek-a-boo.

Sometimes bears
get cross.
They stamp about
and shout.

It's not easy loving bears
when they're like that.

A good thing to do
is to give them a
small snack.
Being cross makes
bears hungry.

If you love a bear
you will know that bears like having baths.
They make big bear waves.

And when they get out they like to be tickled.
It makes them wriggle and
giggle and jiggle.

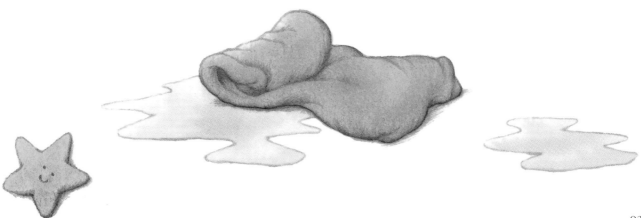

If you love a bear
you will know that bears like to
go to bed when they're sleepy.

They yawn big yawns.

Then they snuggle you up in a soft
cosy blanket and give you bear hugs.

Everyone should have a bear to love.

To Mum with Love

Vivian French

illustrated by

Dana Kubick

It was the day before Mum's birthday.
Stanley went to see his big brother, Rex.
"What are you giving Mum?" he asked.

Good idea

"Flowers," said Rex. "She likes flowers."
"Good idea," said Stanley, and he
hurried off to the garden.

Stanley picked ...   five of the biggest ...

but by the time he got back inside, all the petals had fallen off.

flowers …

that he could see …

- Bother

"Bother," said Stanley, and his ears drooped.

Stanley went to find his big sister, Queenie.
She was counting the money in her
money-box.
"Is that for Mum's present?" Stanley asked.

-Oh!

"Yes," said Queenie. "I'm giving her a tin of
   toffees."
"Oh," said Stanley, and he rushed off to find
   his own money-box.

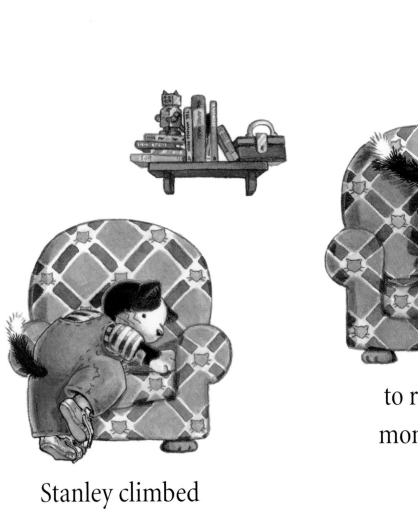

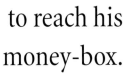

Stanley climbed
up to the shelf …

to reach his
money-box.

but when the
box fell open …

He wanted to buy
Mum toffees too …

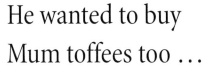

it was empty except for
a piece of jigsaw puzzle.
"Bother," said Stanley, and
his whiskers quivered.

Stanley went to look for his biggest sister, Flora.

"What are you doing?" he asked.

"Making Mum a birthday cake," Flora said.

—Hurrah!

"Hurrah!" said Stanley, and he dashed out of
the kitchen.

Stanley's mud cake ...

ooked …

lovely …

but not for long.
"Bother," said Stanley,
and his tail dragged
behind him.

Stanley went slowly upstairs to look
for a present for Mum. He tipped out his
cardboard box of cars, but there was nothing
that wasn't chipped or dented.

Flora appeared in the doorway.
"Mum says it's bedtime," she said.

That night, Stanley didn't sleep very well.

Early next morning, Flora, Queenie and Rex came
into Stanley's room.

"What's the matter?" Rex asked.

"I haven't got anything for Mum," said Stanley.

"Just give her a kiss," said Flora. "That's what she'd like best."
 Stanley sat bolt upright.
"I know!" he said. "I know what to do."
"Are you coming?" said Queenie.
"In a minute," Stanley said.

Flora, Queenie and Rex went downstairs
to give Mum their presents.
"Flowers!" said Mum. "They're lovely!

And my favourite toffees! And WHAT
a beautiful cake – but where's Stanley?"

Suddenly …

Stanley was standing in the doorway, carrying
his big cardboard box.
"HAPPY BIRTHDAY!" he said.

Mum began to open the box.

"Stanley!" said Rex and Flora and Queenie.

"There's nothing inside!"

"Yes there is!" said Stanley. "It's a box of kisses!
    And I filled it right up to the top!"
"Oh Stanley," said Mum, "it's a wonderful present,"
    and she kissed Stanley's nose.

"Don't use them up all at once," said Rex.
   Mum smiled. "I think boxes of kisses last for
   ever and ever," she said.
"Yes," said Stanley. "For ever and ever and EVER."
   But he gave Mum another kiss – just in case.

LOVE and KISSES

Sarah Wilson ♥ Melissa Sweet

Blow a kiss and let it go.
You never know
how love will grow –

Smooch and smack!
You kiss your cat.
Your cat may kiss a cow.
The cow may kiss a giggling goose,
The goose, a fish – somehow!

The fish - splish! splash! - may kiss a fox.
The fox may kiss a frog.
The frog may jump to plant a kiss
upon a friendly dog.

The dog may kiss a frisky horse
and catch him by surprise!
The horse may kiss a red-winged bird
with twinkles in her eyes.

The bird may fly to kiss a cow,
who'll laugh a great big "Moooo!"
The cow may run to kiss a cat,
who'll then kiss ...

you-know-who!

Kisses! Kisses! Smooch and SMACK!

– you'll have your love and kisses back!

I LOVE YOU
JUST THE WAY YOU ARE

Virginia Miller

One day Bartholomew was grumpy…
His ears were cold.

"Wrap your scarf around your ears
to keep them warm," said George.

But Bartholomew was still grumpy.
His legs felt too stumpy.

"I'll carry you," said George.

At home, Bartholomew's porridge was too lumpy,

his tummy too plumpy,

and he was too small.

"I'll feed you," said George.

At bathtime, Bartholomew hid.

He did not like **anything** at **all**.

141

"What a day," said George.
"You've been so grumpy,
your legs have felt stumpy,
your porridge too lumpy,
your tummy too plumpy
but Ba …"

"I love you
just the way you are."

Bartholomew felt better. He kissed George,

and brushed his teeth all by himself.

"Time for bed, Ba," said George.
"We both need a little rest."

"Nah," said Bartholomew.

Lullaby Lion

Vivian French   illustrated by Alison Bartlett

Little lion

Large lion

Licking lion

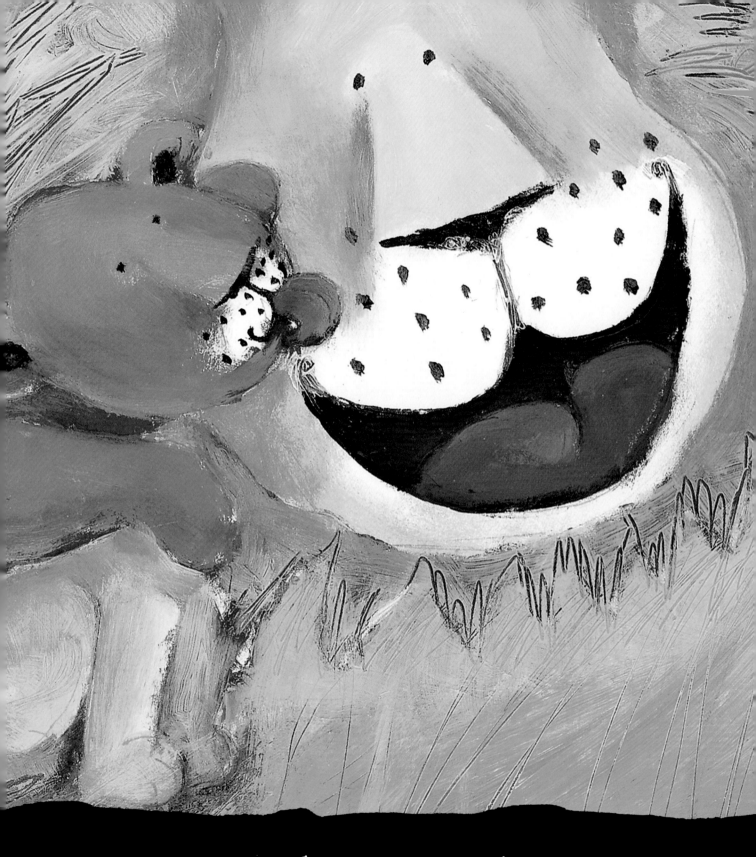

Laughing lion

Lazy lion

Leaping lion

Lost lion

Looking lion

Love you, love

you, Lullaby lion!

Acknowledgements

Each story and poem in this collection
has been previously published by
Walker Books Ltd,
87 Vauxhall Walk,
London SE11 5HJ